P9-BZB-582

Mama Mine, Mama Mine

RITA GRAY
illustrated by PONDER GOEMBEL

Dutton Children's Books

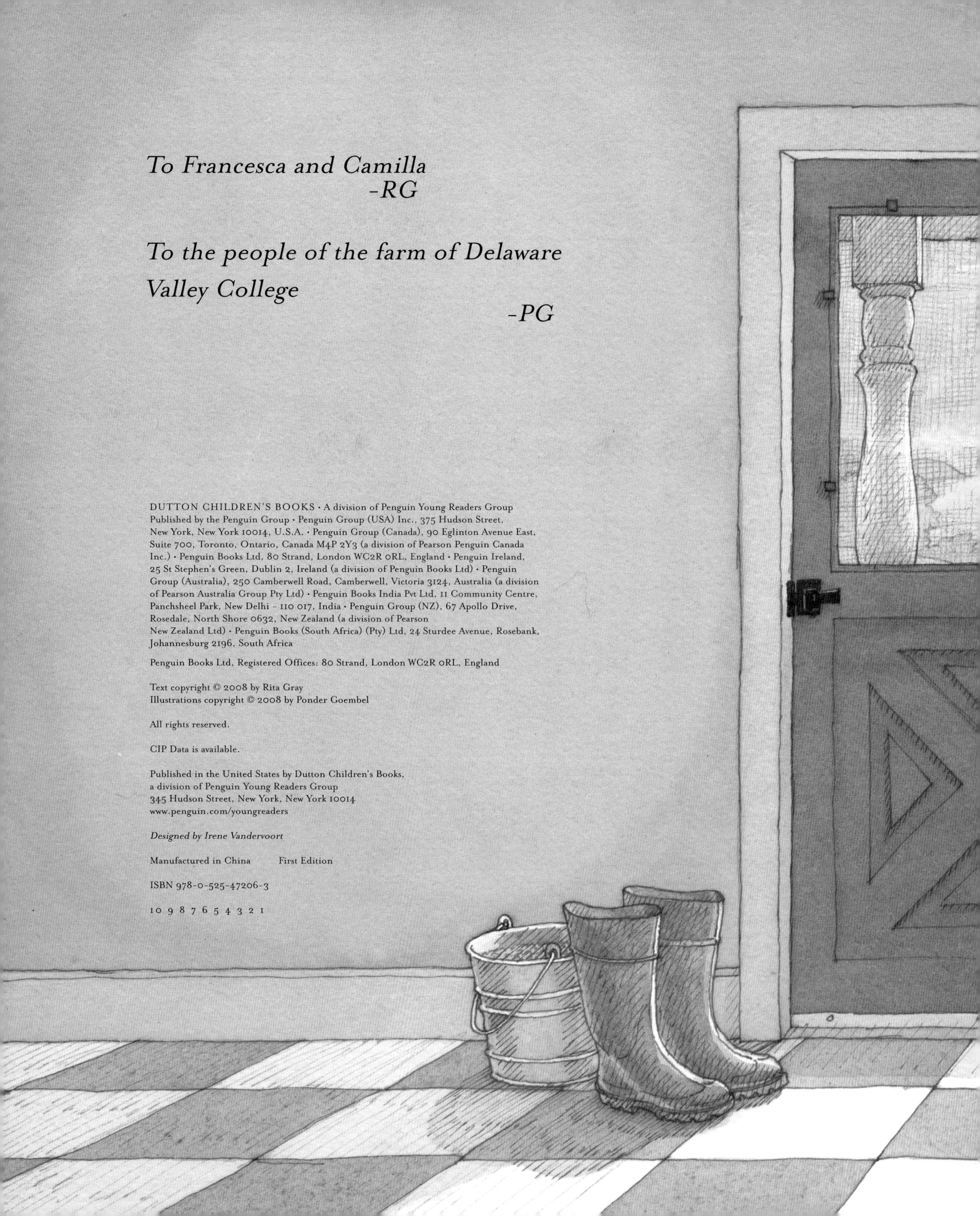

To Francesca and Camilla
-RG

To the people of the farm of Delaware Valley College
-PG

DUTTON CHILDREN'S BOOKS • A division of Penguin Young Readers Group
Published by the Penguin Group • Penguin Group (USA) Inc., 375 Hudson Street, New York, New York 10014, U.S.A. • Penguin Group (Canada), 90 Eglinton Avenue East, Suite 700, Toronto, Ontario, Canada M4P 2Y3 (a division of Pearson Penguin Canada Inc.) • Penguin Books Ltd, 80 Strand, London WC2R 0RL, England • Penguin Ireland, 25 St Stephen's Green, Dublin 2, Ireland (a division of Penguin Books Ltd) • Penguin Group (Australia), 250 Camberwell Road, Camberwell, Victoria 3124, Australia (a division of Pearson Australia Group Pty Ltd) • Penguin Books India Pvt Ltd, 11 Community Centre, Panchsheel Park, New Delhi - 110 017, India • Penguin Group (NZ), 67 Apollo Drive, Rosedale, North Shore 0632, New Zealand (a division of Pearson New Zealand Ltd) • Penguin Books (South Africa) (Pty) Ltd, 24 Sturdee Avenue, Rosebank, Johannesburg 2196, South Africa

Penguin Books Ltd, Registered Offices: 80 Strand, London WC2R 0RL, England

CIP Data is available.

Published in the United States by Dutton Children's Books,
a division of Penguin Young Readers Group
345 Hudson Street, New York, New York 10014
www.penguin.com/youngreaders

Designed by Irene Vandervoort

Manufactured in China First Edition

ISBN 978-0-525-47206-3

10 9 8 7 6 5 4 3 2 1

When will you come back,
Mama hen, mama hen?

After I peck around the pen
And race red rooster, *cock-a-doodle-doo!*
I'll come back, come back to you.

When will you come back,
Mama cow, mama cow?

After I graze beneath the bough
Where grass grows green, *mooo, mooo!*
I'll come back, come back to you.

When will you come back,
Mama cat, mama cat?

After I stalk a big brown rat,
On quiet cat paws, damp with dew,
I'll come back, come back to you.

When will you come back,
Mama pig, mama pig?

After I eat at my trough so big.
I'll chew and chew, and when I'm through,
I'll come back, come back to you.

When will you come back,
Mama mare, mama mare?

After I hold each hoof in the air
For silver shoes, shiny and new,
I'll come back, come back to you.

When will you come back,
Mama sheep, mama sheep?

After my wool is piled in a heap.
After it's shorn, each white curlicue,
I'll come back, come back to you.

When will you come back,
Mama dove, mama dove?

After I soar in the sky above
And call to the clouds, *coo-coo,*
I'll come back, come back to you.

When will you come back,
Mama dog, mama dog?

After I cross the mossy log
And find a stream to splash into,
I'll come back, come back to you.

When will you come back,
Mama duck, mama duck?

After I dabble down in the muck
And nibble reeds, like big ducks do,
I'll come back, come back to you.

When will you come back,
Mama mouse, mama mouse?

After I visit the big farmhouse
And take a pea from last night's stew,
I'll come back, come back to you.

When will you come back,
Mama mine, Mama mine?

After I hang the wash on the line,

And gather wool to spin into yarn,
And see the babies born in the barn.